This book belongs to

_____

Christmas Eve
Published by Createspace
https://www.createspace.com/
ISBN-978-1979345750
ISBN-1979345759

Christmas Eve

Written by L.A. Jones

Illustrated by Leila Nabih

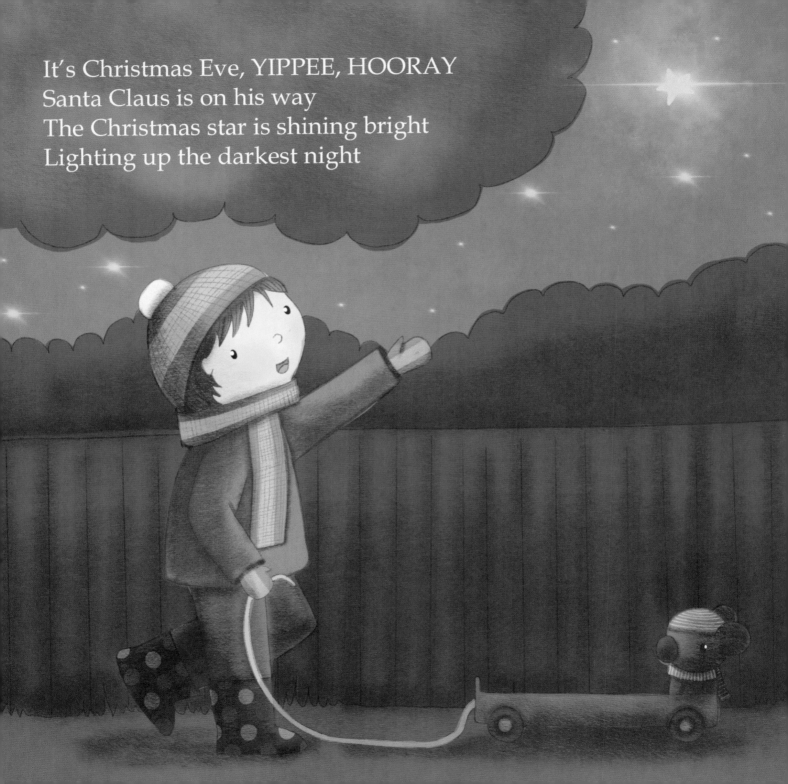

It's Christmas Eve, YIPPEE, HOORAY
Santa Claus is on his way
The Christmas star is shining bright
Lighting up the darkest night

Excitement which one can't contain
The need to shout, to go insane
I have tried, very hard
To be good this year, I kid you not

Flakes of snow begin to fall
Frosted panes, white front lawns
Rudolph's nose can light the way
Even on the foggiest day

I hope Santa received my list
I hope the elves can grant my wish
They work hard, all year round
Making toys that will astound

From bikes to dolls, planes and kites
The elves make everything just right

I want to run, I wish to hop
I want to skip and sing a lot!

Christmas carols, Jingle Bells
Little Donkey, Bethlehem
Our Christmas tree, looks so nice
The stockings hung, oh such delight

Mince pies deep, milk pearly white
Orange carrots, big and bright
Santa's plate looks just right
Awaiting him, this coldest night

I've had my bath, I smell divine
New pyjamas look so fine
I thought this day would never come
It took forever, I was glum

The time for bed is almost nigh
I'm off to brush my pearly whites
Teeth so bright and squeaky clean
Breath that would impress the Queen

Happy now I'll always be
Buzzing wildly like a bee
After all, it's one more sleep
Christmas will be here for keeps

I wonder if Santa is near my street
I wonder if he will leave a treat
Whatever it is, that tomorrow may bring
I will be so grateful, my heart it shall sing

Sweet dreams everybody
Goodnight and God bless
Have a wonderful Christmas
Let's hope it's the best!